Romero

Romero

Published by Modern Publishing,
a Division of Unisystems, Inc.

Copyright © 1986 Victoria House Publishing Ltd.

Designed for Modern Publishing by Victoria
House Publishing Ltd., 4–5 Lower Borough Walls,
Bath, England

® —Honey Bear Books is a trademark owned by
Honey Bear Productions Inc., and is registered in the
U.S. patent and trademark office.

Printed in Belgium

TRIPTUMBLE
THE BEAR

Written by Stewart Cowley
Illustrated by Colin Petty

MODERN PUBLISHING
A Division of Unisystems, Inc.
New York, New York 10022

Triptumble Bear was an eager young cub,
Always rushing wherever he went.
He often tripped and stumbled and tumbled and fell,
Leaving branches all trampled and bent.

Out in the jungle, where he played with his friends,
He'd hurry and then slip right down on the ground.
He'd fall into the creek or bump into a tree,
And his friends would laugh all around.

But Triptumble didn't care what anyone thought,
He didn't care what anyone said.
For his most favorite thing in the world to do,
Was speed around on his bike, that was bright, shiny and red.

"Triptumble dear," his mother would say,
"You really must try to slow down.
With all your rushing and pushing all over the place
Everyone will think you're a clown!"

"A good job is what Triptumble needs!"
His father decided one night.
"Old Ben the Baboon has some work in his store,
For some youngster who's nice and polite."

So Triptumble started the very next day.
But when Mrs. Gorilla stopped by
He hurried and scurried all over the place,
And then *plop!* — he fell into the big apple pie!

"Oh no!" cried Old Ben, "what a terrible mess!"
As Triptumble staggered around,
And stumbled straight into a large stack of cans
That immediately crashed to the ground.

"You can't work in here, but perhaps you could try
To deliver this order instead!"
So Ben filled a box and Triptumble hurried out,
When an idea came into his head.

"I could get this job done in no time at all!"
So he hurried back home with his load.
He put the box in a cart in the back of his bike,
And eagerly pedaled out onto the road.

"Watch where you're going!" cried Jimmy Giraffe.
"Look out!" yelled Tiger Cub Bill.
"I can't stop!" he cried, for he'd lost all control
Of his bike as it sped down the hill.

The bike hit a bump, swerved and rolled through a hedge,
Tipping over by Mrs. Sloth's door.
When Triptumble saw the smashed grocery box
He moaned, "Oh no, I'm in trouble for sure!"

Sammy Sloth and his mother rushed out in alarm,
To see what the noise was about.
When Sam reached the door he covered his eyes,
And Mrs. Sloth simply started to shout.

"Sammy's birthday party is today," cried Mrs. Sloth,
"All the guests will be here at three!"
Young Sammy Sloth just sat down and wailed,
"Now there'll be no party for me!"

Triptumble felt sad, he felt much worse than bad,
To have ruined the birthday party for young Sam.
"I'll run back to the store, and get all new supplies.
I can't tell you how sorry I am!"

"What's come over Triptumble?" the animals asked,
When they saw Triptumble pedal safely down the lane.
Triptumble got more groceries from Mr. Baboon,
And promised never to be careless again.

Triptumble still rushes but not quite as fast,
And he does his work with more care.
When he takes his friends for rides their parents all say,
"They're quite safe, they're with Triptumble Bear!"